Dear Parents and Educators,

Welcome to Penguin Young Readers! As parents and educators, you know that each child develops at his or her own pace—in terms of speech, critical thinking, and, of course, reading. Penguin Young Readers recognizes this fact. As a result, each Penguin Young Readers book is assigned a traditional easy-to-read level (1–4) as well as a Guided Reading Level (A–P). Both of these systems will help you choose the right book for your child. Please refer to the back of each book for specific leveling information. Penguin Young Readers features esteemed authors and illustrators, stories about favorite characters, fascinating nonfiction, and more!

Tiny Goes to the Library

LEVEL 1
GUIDED READING LEVEL D

This book is perfect for an **Emergent Reader** who:
- can read in a left-to-right and top-to-bottom progression;
- can recognize some beginning and ending letter sounds;
- can use picture clues to help tell the story; and
- can understand the basic plot and sequence of simple stories.

Here are some **activities** you can do during and after reading this book:
- Picture Clues: Use the pictures to tell the story. "Read" the illustrations.
- Make Connections: Why is Tiny upset he cannot go into the library? Have you ever felt left out?
- Sight Words: Sight words are frequently used words that readers must know just by looking at them. These words are not "sounded out" or "decoded"; rather they are known instantly, on sight. Knowing these words helps children develop into efficient readers. The words listed below are sight words used in this book. As you read or reread the story, have the child point out the sight words.

for	go	here	no	the
get	good	my	stop	you

Remember, sharing the love of reading with a child is the best gift you can give!

—Bonnie Bader, EdM, and Katie Carella, EdM
    Penguin Young Readers program

*Penguin Young Readers are leveled by independent reviewers applying the standards developed by Irene Fountas and Gay Su Pinnell in *Matching Books to Readers: Using Leveled Books in Guided Reading*, Heinemann, 1999.

For Judy, the best editor
in the whole wide world—CM

To Angie, my wife and best friend: I'm so
glad God brought us together to make a
home. I love you!—RD

Penguin Young Readers
Published by the Penguin Group
Penguin Group (USA) Inc., 375 Hudson Street, New York, New York 10014, USA
Penguin Group (Canada), 90 Eglinton Avenue East, Suite 700, Toronto, Ontario M4P 2Y3, Canada
(a division of Pearson Penguin Canada Inc.)
Penguin Books Ltd., 80 Strand, London WC2R 0RL, England
Penguin Group Ireland, 25 St. Stephen's Green, Dublin 2, Ireland (a division of Penguin Books Ltd.)
Penguin Group (Australia), 250 Camberwell Road, Camberwell, Victoria 3124, Australia
(a division of Pearson Australia Group Pty. Ltd.)
Penguin Books India Pvt. Ltd., 11 Community Centre, Panchsheel Park, New Delhi—110 017, India
Penguin Group (NZ), 67 Apollo Drive, Rosedale, Auckland 0632, New Zealand
(a division of Pearson New Zealand Ltd.)
Penguin Books (South Africa) (Pty.) Ltd., 24 Sturdee Avenue,
Rosebank, Johannesburg 2196, South Africa

Penguin Books Ltd., Registered Offices: 80 Strand, London WC2R 0RL, England

Text copyright © 2000 by Cari Meister. Illustrations copyright © 2000 by Rich Davis. All rights reserved.
First published in 2000 by Viking and Puffin Books, imprints of Penguin Group (USA) Inc. Published in
2011 by Penguin Young Readers, an imprint of Penguin Group (USA) Inc., 345 Hudson Street,
New York, New York 10014. Manufactured in China.

Library of Congress Control Number: 98-051134

ISBN 978-0-14-130488-5   10 9 8 7 6 5

PENGUIN YOUNG READERS

LEVEL

1

EMERGENT
READER

Tiny Goes to the Library

by Cari Meister
illustrated by Rich Davis

Penguin Young Readers
An Imprint of Penguin Group (USA) Inc.

This is Tiny.

He is my best friend.

He goes where I go.

If I go to the park,

Tiny comes, too.

If I go to the lake,

Tiny comes, too.

Today we
are going to
the library.

I get my library card.

I get my wagon.

Time to go!

Sorry, Tiny.

No dogs in the library.

You wait here.

I go inside.

Tiny stays outside.

I get dog books.

I get frog books.

I get bird books for Tiny.

I fill the wagon.

Tiny helps.

Oh no! Too many books!

I cannot pull the wagon.

Tiny can!

Stop, Tiny, stop!

Wait for me!

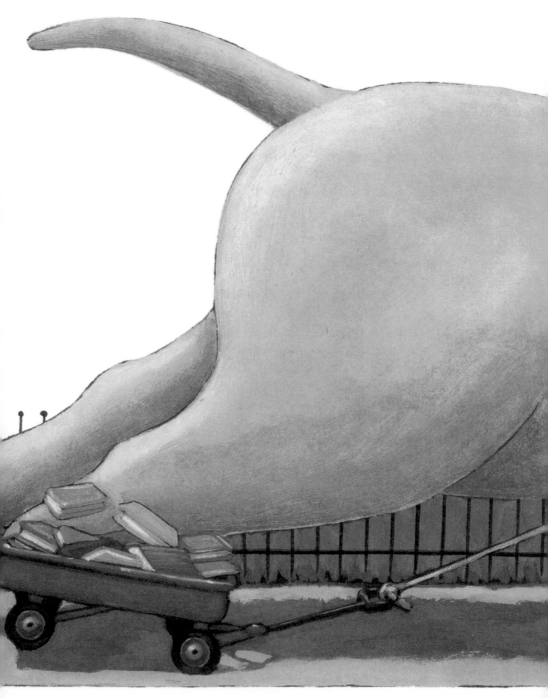

Go, Tiny, go!

Good dog, Tiny.